THIS BLOOMSBURY BOOK

BELONGS TO

....

EVEN MONSTERS NEED HAIRCUTS

Matthew McElligott

BLOOMSBURY

LONDON BERLIN NEW YORK

To Christy and Anthony, and to Frank Hodge,
who for twenty-seven years faithfully opened his store every
full moon so the monsters could come in and pick out a book

Bloomsbury Publishing, London, Berlin and New York

First published in Great Britain in October 2010 by Bloomsbury Publishing Plc
36 Soho Square, London, W1D 3QY

First published in the USA in 2010 by Walker Publishing Company, Inc,
a division of Bloomsbury Publishing, Inc

A CIP catalogue record of this book is available from the British Library

ISBN 978 1 4088 1393 5

1 3 5 7 9 10 8 6 4 2

Printed in China by Printplus Limited, Shenzhen, Guangdong

All papers used by Bloomsbury Publishing are natural, recyclable products made from
wood grown in well-managed forests. The manufacturing processes conform to the
environmental regulations of the country of origin

www.bloomsbury.com

My dad is a barber.
I like to watch him work.
I'm a barber too.

Tonight will be a full moon.
I'll need to get to bed early.

Just before midnight, I hear a soft tapping sound.
Vlad is waiting for me at the window.

I grab my pack and climb down the tree. Together, we cross the fields into town.

I am not allowed out of the house alone.

But I am not alone. Vlad is with me.

Soon we arrive at the alley behind
the shop. I have a skeleton key.

I unpack my supplies. The rotting tonic, horn polish and stink wax go on the counter. The shamp-*ewww* goes next to the sink.

I tuck the moon powder into my pocket, right next to my tangling brush. I'm ready to begin.

Around twelve thirty, Igor wanders in.

By one o'clock, the shop is full.
It's going to be a busy night.

Some customers are easy.

Some are more difficult.

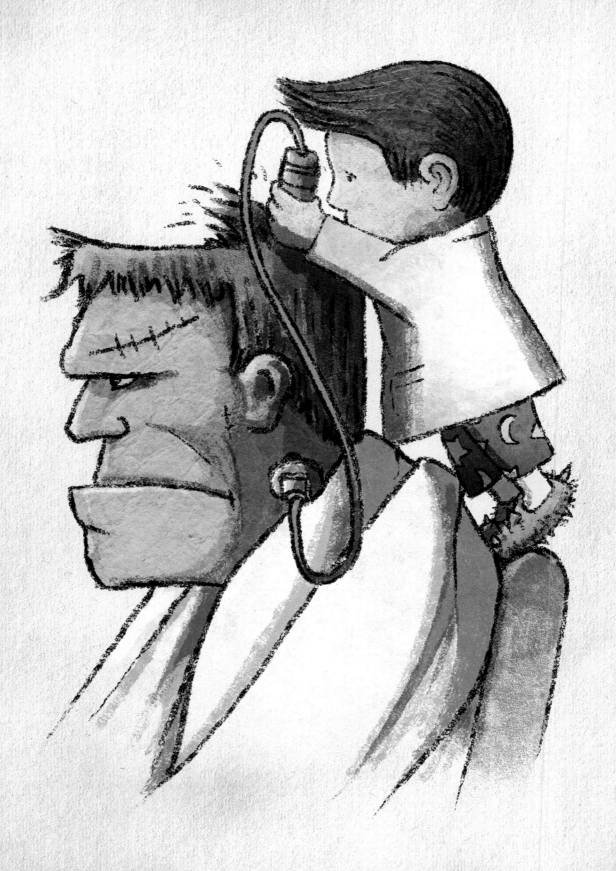

Some always get the same thing.

Some always want to try something new.

And with some customers, it's tough to know exactly what they want.

Things are going well. Everyone is
getting along. And then it happens.
There is a knock at the front door.
No one ever knocks on the front door.
They all know to come in the back.
Who could it be?

It is a customer. A *human* customer.
We have never had a human customer before.
What are we going to do?

Nobody moves as the man walks to the barber chair.

I am nervous. More nervous than I have
ever been. And then he asks me . . .

'Can you take a little off the top?'

We all have a good laugh over that one.

The sun will be up soon, and the monsters have to go. We sweep up the shop.

We flip back the pictures and turn out the lights. It's important that we don't leave *anything* behind.

Some of the guys give me a ride
home.
'See you next month!' I shout.

Soon my dad will be waking up
to go to work. He has his own
customers to take care of.

After all, even humans need haircuts.

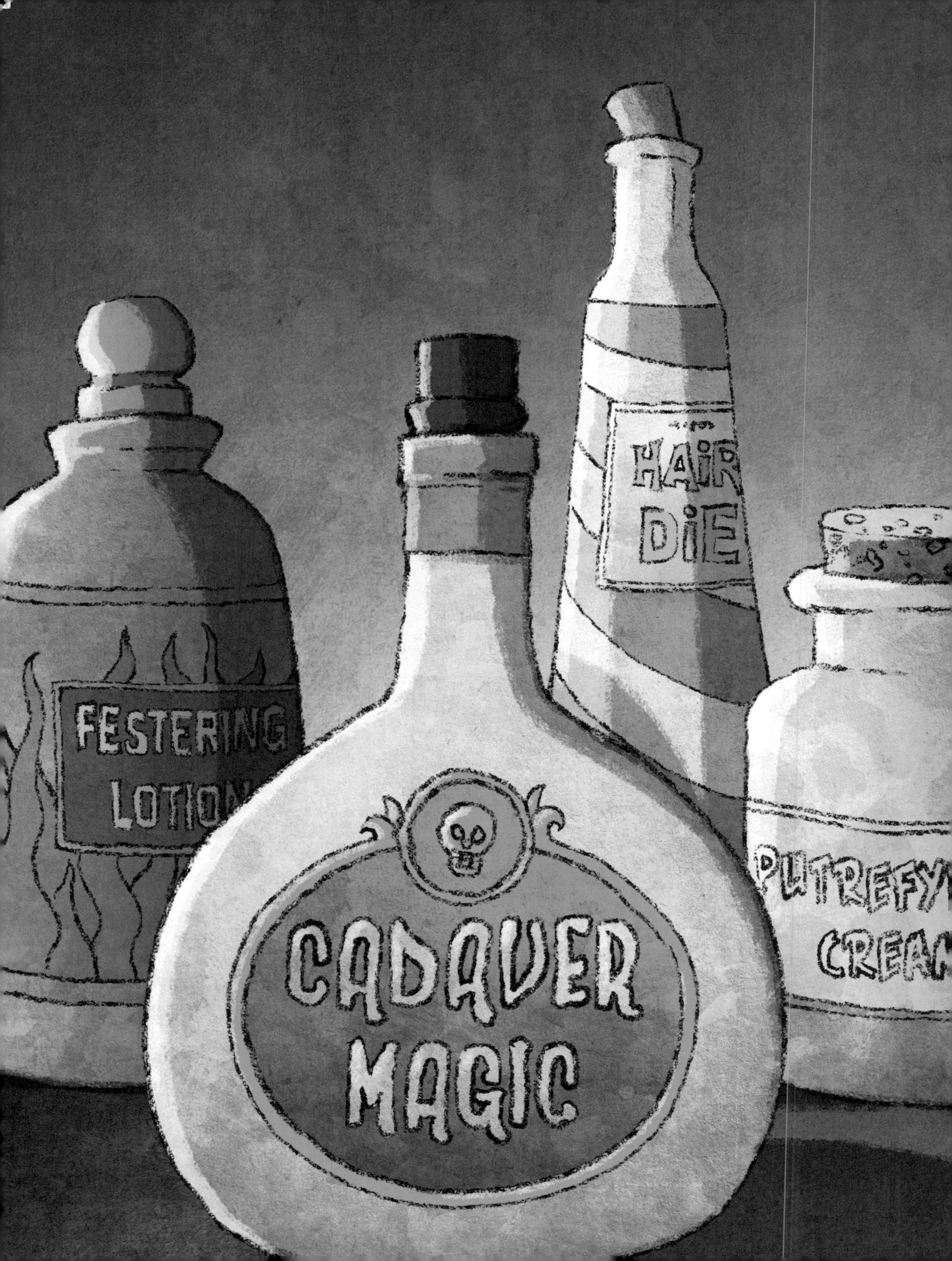

FESTERING
LOTION
HAIR
DIE
CADAVER
MAGIC

More raucous adventures
for little monsters everywhere...

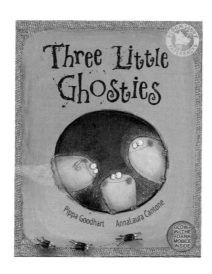

Three Little Ghosties
By Pippa Goodhart
& illustrated by AnnaLaura Cantone

The Everyday Witch
By Liz Martinez
& illustrated by Mark Beech

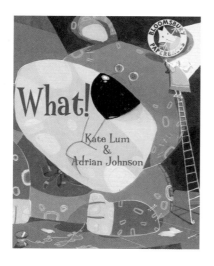

What!
By Adrian Johnson
& illustrated by Kate Lum

Night of the
Veggie Monster
By George McClements